Wearing white on Labor Day

Karen Ligocki

ISBN: 978-1-963949-98-8 (Paperback)

Printed in the United States of America

To the fans that had helped in the funding to have this book published. Through trying time, thank you for having my back.

Also, to the many fans that purchase my books, my supporters even if you are not readers and just cheer me on.

My family, that keeps me grounded.

Let's not forget my furry therapist

Cody and Riley.

Thank you all.

Contents

Chapter 1 1

Chapter 2 4

Chapter 3 9

Chapter 4 15

Chapter 5 19

Chapter 6 23

Chapter 7 28

Chapter 8 32

Chapter 9 36

Chapter 10 39

Chapter 11 43

Chapter 12 49

Chapter 13 54

Chapter 14 57

Chapter 15 60

Chapter 16 63

Chapter 17 66

Chapter 18 69

Chapter 19 73

Chapter 20 79

Chapter 1

Dorie was getting breakfast, and her kids Scott, Katie and Noah were up early. They wanted to go riding. Her father Paul had stables built on Dorie's brother Jesse's land. Paul moved in with Jesse from Minnesota after his wife passed. Now, Dorie and the kids are staying here in Poland, Maine, with them til she gets on her feet.

Dorie left Minnesota after her divorce. Her husband was gone, given up parental rights and moved to Alaska.

"Mom, how come you don't take us to the stables anymore?" Dorie's oldest, Scott, asked.

"Well, honey, it's just that I have so much to do around here. "

" Mr Max asks about you all the time, Mom." Katie shared.

Max, yeah, well, as much as she did like Max, Dorie saw him with a woman. It seemed like it was more than friendly. Dorie was not ready to get her heart strung along again. Her divorce, even though almost 2 years ago, was still fresh in her mind.

" That's nice, Katie. You can tell Mr Max Mommy is doing just fine."

" …Or you could come with us and tell him yourself," her father said as he walked into the kitchen. " Good morning everyone."

The cheers went up for Grandpa. Paul recently retired from The Maine State Police. Paul loved being home now; he adored his grandchildren, and they adored him.

" Maybe some other day. I'm just not up to it today."

Paul let out a sigh. He knew Dorie had feelings for Max but did not know what happened. I am not going to push her, Paul thought to himself.

" How's everything moving along with the BBQ?"

Dorie smiled, grateful that her father was not going to push the issue. Labor Day was in a week, and the Wiseman's were throwing their annual Wear White for Labor Day BBQ. The challenge was the food. It was the messiest of messiest, and the games were tug of war, flag football, and egg toss... you got dirty.

" It looks like everything is going in the right direction, dad."

" Grandpa, can we go to horsies now." Little Noah, of course, was guided by his siblings.

 Paul winked at Dorie.

" Noah, I'm afraid it's just me and you today since you asked."

Scotty and Katie started to protest.

" Come on, let's get a move on."

Tiny and Moose, Jesse's girlfriend Maddie's dogs, raced to the car. Dorie laughed.

" You got the whole gang. We can talk about the BBQ when you get home."

Off they went.

Dorie missed her brother Benny, and Benny was a federal agent. He came to Jesse's on the 3rd of July.

The case he was on ended, and Benny showed up at the town independence celebration, Summer Blast. Thinking that he had enough of police work, Benny decided he too, was going to stay in Poland. Benny had started dating an EMT named Oliver, whom he met at Summer Blast. It wasn't enough, though. By the end of July, Benny missed being out there undercover. He missed the hum of the city, catching the bad guys. When his lead agent called, Benny knew he had to go back. When Benny told Oliver, they had a huge argument and Benny left the next day.

Maddie, Jesse's girlfriend, who once was a lead reporter for the local paper, but left to per-sue

her dream of writing series books. Maddie came out into the kitchen and grabbed a cup of coffee.

" Morning, Dorie."

" Morning, Mads, there's some scrambled eggs and bacon, still warm."

Maddie got up and got the eggs and bacon. She noticed Dorie was a little down.

" You okay, Dorie?"

Dorie smiled weakly.

" Yeah, Yeah, just missing Benny.

I guess I just wish he'd had settled down."

" That's all?" Maddie had sensed that Dorie liked Max but, for some reason, stopped going to the stables.

" Katie said Max asked about me," Dorie told Maddie what she saw.

"Dorie, it could have been anyone."

" I don't know, it didn't seem like that. I don't want to get in the middle. I don't need to get hurt again."

" I understand."

The two women turned their conversation to food for the bbq.

Chapter 2

Paul and the kids got down to the stables. Max was out front with a pretty lady. Paul knew that Dorie had been taking a liking to Max, that made Paul happy, he loved Max like a son.

Paul also sensed Max having some feelings towards Dorie, the looks across the dining table when Max came for supper. Something happened, though, after the Fourth of July, Dorie's whole attitude changed. Paul wanted to ask her what was going on but somehow thought better of it. His kids always came to him when they needed to talk or a sounding board. I'll let her be.

"Hey Paul"

" Max, good to see you, and who is this lovely lady?

" This is Tammy. You told me to hire a hand to help out. Tammy is the best. Knows horses, inside and out."

" Nice to meet you, Mr. Wiseman."

" Paul, please, the pleasures all mine."

A little tug on Paul's sleeve reminded him why he was there.

" Oh, and these are my grandkid

Scotty, Katie and Noah"

Tammy kneeled down.

" Hello, do you guys ride? " the kids nodded. " well, then let's go."

The kids didn't need any more encouragement. They ran to the horses. Tammy got up and said to Paul.

" I can set them up for you, Noah rides with you? "

" Yup"

Tammy left the two men.

" Pretty girl."

Max looked at Paul, then laughed.

" I hadn't noticed."

" Come on, Max."

" She's my cousin, we grew up together like brother and sister."

" Max, was she around here the days after the Fourth of July?

"Yeah, she's been staying with me til she finds a place of her own."

It was Paul's turn to laugh.

" Paul, what's so funny?"

"Nothing, nothing. Can you bring Tammy up to sign some paperwork and maybe come for supper tomorrow? "

"I dunno, Paul, I don't think Dorie wants me around."

"Son, just come, I'll take care of Dorie."

When Paul got over to Tammy and the kids, Paul did a double take.

Little Noah was on a little pony, and with the help of Tammy, he was all saddled up on... Paul wasn't sure about that. This was not one of his.

" Noah! Did you buy a pony?"

The little boy went into a fit of giggles. Max came over.

" The pony is mine, Paul. That is Cinnamon, a local farmer who was practically giving them away. I got 5. I was hoping to rent the five spare stables, but I'd understand if…"

" You are not renting the stables, please. You are like family. Just look how happy that little boy is!"

Noah's grin was ear to ear as Tammy held him up. Scotty and Katie were each on the pony they had been riding since coming from Minnesota.

"Thanks, Paul."

"Tammy, I am building a home in this area. I planned on building some cabins. Suppose you don't mind staying at Max' for awhile. You are more than welcome to use one of the cabins for housing."

" As long as you let me pay rent,

I like to earn my keep."

" Well, yeah, of course. We will work something out. Now, I have an idea. I want to play a joke on my daughter."

Paul's joke was for the cousins to come to supper and introduce Tammy, but only by name. If anyone asks, avoid the question.

The cousins looked at each other.

" I dunno, Paul, Dorie is still hurting from the divorce. Her emotions are pretty raw."

"Max, she didn't talk to you all summer over jealousy. She might get mad, but I know my daughter.. she'll be okay."

Max looked at Tammy.

" Okay, but the first sign she's upset.. "

Paul interrupted, " We tell her."

Paul gathered up the kids and dogs and went home.

Noah ran into the house, straight to Dorie.

" Mama, I ride horsie by myself."

Dorie made a surprise face.

" You did?"

All three kids told Dorie about their day at once.

" Hey, Dorie," Dorie looked at her father. " Max is coming for supper tomorrow. I want to make Chili. Do we have everything in the house, or do I need to stop at the store in the morning?"

" Why is Max coming tomorrow?"

" He hired a hand. I thought it would be the neighborly thing to do."

"Oh, okay,"

Scotty piped in. " You'll love Tammy, Mama, she fun."

Tammy, she?

" Okay."

Paul knew that it was anything but okay. He saw all the emotions run through Dorie's eyes. Abort joke, thought to himself. He made a quick call to Max to forget the joke and just come up for supper tomorrow.

"Thank God, Tammy was a little uncomfortable but didn't want to say. She didn't want to hurt Tammy's feelings."

Paul liked Tammy even more after that, and respect goes a long way.

Jesse watched his sister at supper time. Dorie is usually chatty and asks everyone about their day. Lynne, Paul's fiance, asked Dorie twice if she was feeling okay.

" I'm okay Lynne, I'm just tired, is all, been a long day."

" Well, you go in the parlor and rest yourself, me and your dad can clean up."

Dorie went into the other room. A little time passed, and Jesse and Maddie came in.

" All right, Dorie spill," Jesse said.

Dorie opened her eyes.

"Spill what?"

" What's going on? Why are you so quiet?"

" I'm just tired, Jesse. The BBQ is this weekend, then Dad invited Max and some woman he hired to come for supper. I know you must think I twiddle my thumbs all…"

Jesse looked at Maddie and nodded.

" You know you make enough food to feed an army and their families. You only have to set to places more. So I'll ask again, what's up Dor? I'm sensing something to do with Max .. like maybe the woman."

" Wow! Sheriff, you have been sensing again?"

Dorie knew it was a jerky thing to say, but she really did have a headache and really was tired.

Jesse and Maddie laughed.

" I'm sorry, Jess. I really am tired, and I do have a headache."

Maddie reached out to Dorie, taking her hands.

" Honey, your dad forgot to mention that the girl coming with Max is his cousin. "

" So you do like Max?"

" This one, he should have been detective, you know."

" My sister and my friend, I feel like Ross on 'Friends".

They all laughed.

Maddie looked Dorie in the eyes.

" You better tell Max now, Dorie. God knows how much they like to gossip at the Sheriff's."

"Jeez, this must be zingers for Jesse day."

Chapter 3

Andy loved working at Hole in the Wall Hobbies. His co-owner and friend Ray made working like a day at the toy store or the mall, going into great detail about one item or another. Andy loved it. Once he left the paper, the stress fell away. He loved being editor-in-chief, but with all the deadlines and paperwork, he lost all the passion.

Andy recently found out he was diabetic. Being a health nut, that was a pretty surprising diagnosis. With the right medication and his lifestyle changes with less stress, Andy felt the best he's been in awhile.

He started dating Vee a couple of months ago. He was crazy about her. Never a dull moment with Vee around. She loved to laugh and make people laugh, and she was funny as heck.

I can't wait to bring her to the Wiseman's Labor Day barbecue,

I picture her, getting right in the middle of Jesse's family, Andy thought to himself. Andy could also picture himself settling down with Vee. He didn't want to rush into things, but they got along so well together.

"Will ya stop dreaming about your girl? There's a customer."

Andy chuckled. Ray thought of himself as the boss, probably because Andy was new. Andy actually comes to think of the older man, as a father figure.

" Hi, I'm Andy. Is there anything I can help you with?"

The guy looked up. " ANDY!"

The two men embraced.

" Drew, how are you? What are you doing around here?"

Drew was one of Andy's BU buddies.

" Vacation. The wife wanted to visit her family, and she wanted me to grab a couple of trinkets. "

" Have you seen Anthony?" Andy missed hanging with his friends and hasn't seen a few for awhile.

"Yeah, he found himself a girl. Expect an invite soon."

"Me too. I've been dating a nice girl. We really seem to hit it off. I don't want to scare her off, tho, so going slow."

" What happened at the paper?"

So Andy told Drew all the details about how he became partners with Ray.

" As long as you're happy, Andy, that's what matters."

They caught up a little bit more, then Andy asked, " What are you looking for, your in-laws?"

" Her father likes fishing, and her mom likes things like cross stitching."

Andy called Ray over, introduced the two men and told Ray what Drew was looking for.

" I have just the things. Come on, let's go find them." Drew started to walk away with Ray, then turned.

" Hey Andy, don't be a stranger. Come down to Boston. We have the room. It would be fun."

Andy nodded.

Boston is another thing that Andy missed. Some of the best times in his life happened in Boston, hanging with the guys, all great places to go, Bruins games (once an NHL prospect, Andy was very much into the hockey scene, then blew out his knee.), and he met Jesse in Boston, on campus. It was actually pretty funny that Andy and Jesse both landed in Poland, ME. Like Jesse liked to say, "Who da thunk!" Who indeed.

Drew came over to say goodbye to Andy. It was hard saying goodbye.

"Get your ass down to Boston, me, you and Anthony can find one of those fancy bars to hang out in."

With a wave to Andy and Ray, Drew was gone.

" Nice fella," Ray said.

" One of the best."

" What made you move to Maine?"

" I loved the quiet. I sometimes miss the hum of the city. Waking up to complete silence is wonderful."

"Ha! Wait til you and your girl have kids. Never be quiet again."

Right on cue, Ray's son Frank came in.

" Hi Andy, Dad, you ready."

" See what I mean?"

Andy laughed.

" See you tomorrow, kid."

" Bye, Ray, see ya, Frank."

Vee and I with kids, now that's something to think about.

The door opened, and Andy yelled out.

" Be with you in a minute."

Andy came out from the back room.

" Hello, what can I do for you?"

The woman turned around.

Andy felt like he was punched in the stomach. In a low whisper "Stella."

Stella Cora was " that girl."

Head cheerleader, prom Queen, homecoming Queen. Stella was smart, beautiful, kind, and funny.

Stella broke Andy's heart. Just 18, Andy thought he was going to marry her after college and even had a ring on layaway. One day, Stella told Andy he didn't match her "goals" and that she wanted more than he was offering. Stella broke his heart in a million pieces, shattered it.

Andy went on to Boston University, majoring in journalism. He moved up to Poland and worked his way up to Chief Editor of the Sanford Sentinel. Only recently, Andy lost passion with the paper, and became partners with his friend Ray.

Looking at Stella now was a gut punch. That young cheerleader went on to be a big-time hairstylist on Newbury Street in Boston. Stella was even more beautiful and now was standing in front of him.

"Hello Andy."

Andy nodded, words escaping him. Slowly, seductively, Stella moved a crossed the floor to greet him with a kiss. Andy put his hands on her shoulders to keep her at a distance.

"Chicken?" Stella laughed, a new laugh, breathy and low, not her childhood laugh, sweet and loud.

" Taken, don't need the gossip mills turning. Why are you here?"

" I come to see you. I got word you were working here. I took a ride up with some friends."

" Why did you want to see me?"

" For old time's sake."

" I'm sorry, Stella, I don't want to see you, so either buy something or leave."

"Wow." she paused. "Wow. Is that what you think of me now?"

" You broke my heart, Stel. I don't think of you at all."

" I don't know, Andy, that wasn't the reaction I saw when you saw me."

Andy laughed.

"Time for you to go."

Picking up a random toy.

" How much is this?"

" one hundred dollars."

" For this piece of junk?"

" Everything in this store is antique or collectible. Still want it? I'll ring it up so you can leave."

" If I buy this whole shelf, will you talk to me?"

"That's over $3,000., I'd ring up your sale and tell you to have a good day."

" You'd pass up a $3,000 sale just to get rid of me? Why? We were kids, we broke up, it happens."

" I have a serious girlfriend, Stella. There's no reason for me to talk to you. Now, I talked to you, that will be $3,895. Plus tax. I'll get you a box."

She got out her credit card, and Andy rang up the sale. Stella walked to the door.

" Hey, what about your purchases?"

" Throw them in the trash."

Dorie was a mess, she knew. She needed to pull it together. The food for the BBQ was set, and tables and chairs were waiting to be set up. Jesse and Andy were going to set up the games after supper

tonight. Andy and Vee were coming for supper then the boys would do some work in the yard.

Dorie made Andy's favorite lazy man lasagna. Dorie's problem was Max and his lady friend were coming tomorrow, even though her father was shopping and cooking everything, Dorie was so anxious about it.

The lasagna smelled delicious. The aroma filled the whole house.

There was a knock at the door.

Dorie went and opened it.

" Vee! You're early, where's Andy?"

" He's on his way. He got stuck at the shop, something about a last-minute sale. He sounded weird. I walked over so I could see if you needed any help."

" I'm pretty much all set. I baked some fresh French bread. Your boy will be happy. You would think it's his birthday."

The women laughed. Andy was diabetic. He's been eating small potions lately. Dorie actually went and found a recipe that was diabetic friendly and made her traditional and a small diabetic one for Andy to test.

Chapter 4

Everyone was stuffed with lasagna and fresh French bread. " Come on, let's go sit in the parlor before we go to work in the yard. We will still have some daylight, so let's take a rest."

Paul said, grabbing his youngest grandson like a football and spiking him on the sofa. " Touchdown."

Noah squealed, " GRANDPA!"

" Dad, if he throws up, you're cleaning it. "

Jesse ran up behind Dorie, picked her up and threw her on the love seat. Everyone laughed.

Dorie laughed, too. It felt good, it's been so long, she was afraid she had forgotten how.

They all sat around talking. The mood was light and carefree until Jesse asked Paul, where has Max' been? Dorie excused herself and started to get up.

" Freeze. Okay, Dorie, spill it. What did you do to Max?"

Maddie thrust her elbow into Jesse's ribs. "Ow."

" Leave Dorie alone."

" For your information, brother dear, I didn't touch Max," Dorie said.

Andy said under his breathe

" Maybe that's the problem. "

Vee kicked Andy in the shin.

" Ow"

Paul was laughing so hard and said, " We better get outside before Andy and Jesse can't walk."

"Har har har. "

The guys went into the back yard to start to set up. The BBQ was in two days.

The ladies went into the kitchen,

Lynne went over to Dorie and gave her a hug.

"I know I keep asking this, honey, but are you okay?"

" I don't know, Lynne. Obviously, everyone knows I like Max, but there is something that stops me from moving forward. I'm stuck in first gear,"

" Well, what could it be? Is it Scott?" Vee asked.

" I don't think so. I put Scott in my rare view mirror. He deserves nothing from me. I should have put him in jail.. but the kids, you know." Lynne nodded as said.

" Well, are you afraid to be in a relationship again? It should be easier for you. Max is a great guy. You already hit it off."

Maddie deadpanned. " .. and he's hot!"

They all agreed, laughing.

Jesse walked in.

" Maddie, don't brag about your hot hubby-to-be. They are gonna get jealous."

Dorie and Jesse were always close, even more so now.

" Maddie, you didn't tell us you found a new man."

" Who you girls yakking about?"

The three ladies clammed up.

But Jesse knew who.

" Ohhhh, you are talking about that sexy farm-hand."

Vee looked at Jesse innocently.

"You think the farm hand is sexy?"

Lynne almost choked on her drink.

" Zing"

" Okay, okay, I just came to get some beer."

Dorie passed Jesse 3 beers

" One more, please."

Dorie grabbed another.

" You gonna be peeing all afternoon."

"Not for me. " Jesse batted his eye lashes on his way out.

" The sexy farm hand is helping

us." Laughing out the door.

Dorie blew out a breath.

Maddie went over and put her arms around Dorie.

"Come on, Dor, it's just Max."

"I know, Maddie, I don't even understand it."

"It's hard to move forward, Dorie," Lynne said.

"Yeah, you should have seen me when Jesse decided to babysit me after the attacks." Maddie was struck by a police baton when a woman was terrorizing the citizens of Poland.

" Well, the best I can do is just go with the flow."

Dorie went to turn around and slammed right into the sexy farm hand.

" oh my gosh, Max, I'm so sorry, I wasn't paying attention. "

" I brought more beer. Jesse told me to put it in the fridge. You okay? I didn't mean to startle you. Hi Ladies."

" Hi, Max," Lynne, Vee and Maddie said, the three giggling and smiling like schoolgirls.

" Forgive my family, Max. They are all weirdos."

Max smiled and put the beer in the fridge.

" You ladies ought to be outside. It's a beautiful day."

Maddie and Lynne made their excuses but told Dorie to go outside and sit with the kids.

" Sit? I'm going to put her to work! "

"Where are my manners, Max did you eat yet? There's lasagna. I can heat you a piece and bring it out to you."

" I ate, but I am not passing up Dorie's famous lasagna!"

" Okay, I'll be out in a minute."

Max went out.

Maddie looked at Dorie.

" I don't get it. You are so relaxed around him."

" I thought you two were going to work?"

Lynne laughed.

" Yeah, I'm going to call in that I'm on duty… and spy out the window."

" My new novel can wait another day. I'm gonna spy, too!"

" Oh no, you two are coming out to help. Either cook some stuff for BBQ or come help outside."

Before Vee said anything, Dorie motioned for the door.

" Ugggghhh"

"Fine, she's so bossy."

Dorie laughed at Maddie's response.

" Now, you sound like my kids."

Dorie grabbed the lasagna and led everyone outside.

Chapter 5

Somehow when Dorie woke up this morning, she knew she was in for a bad day, but if you told her, her ex-husband would be in the middle of her family's backyard. She'd have called you nuts.

"DORIE." Scott bellowed, "Tell them to let me see my kids."

Jesse pulled his gun, but Lynne was quicker. " Put it down, Sheriff. I got this."

With daggers in his eyes at Scott, Jesse lowered his weapon. Lynne turned to Paul.

" Behave."

Paul rolled his eyes but was tense. Dorie was anything but relaxed.

" Your kids? I don't see any of your kids here, Scott. Now, if I were you, I'd leave, or I'll call the law. Oh wait, they are already here."

Lynne had called in back up, who were now arriving.

" I just want to talk to them, Dorie. You can't keep them from me."

Dorie ran into the house and came back out with papers.

" These papers say I can, so since this is not my property. I will let my brother, the Sheriff, tell you."

Jesse stepped up into Scott's face.

" Get off my land, or I'll have you escorted off."

Scott hauled off to hit Jesse, but Max dove for his legs.

Maddie had taken the kids out of there before much was seen by them.

Max and Scott were rolling around on the ground. Scott screamed at Max, "Who do you think you are?" Then to Dorie.

" I'm going to take you to court, Dorie. I'll get the best lawyer to get custody back."

Now, it was Dorie's turn. She pulled Max off of Scott. Scott scuttled to his feet.

" Wait, Max, stop." Dorie has had it, she knew this day was coming.

"Did you just threaten me, Scott?"

"What are you going to do about it, Dorie? I'll find the best Custody lawyer around. I'll bring you to your knees, and you will never see those kids again. You are weak."

Paul and Jesse laughed.

All eyes went to them.

"Don't much about the woman, who was your wife, do you Scott? " Paul laughed.

" What are you talking about?"

Jesse looked Scott right in the eye. " You see, before Dorie met you, she was heading to be one of the biggest Family court lawyers around. They predicted she would be one of the youngest judges had she continued. Then she met you. All she wanted her whole life was a family. She gave it all up."

Paul now pulled his gun, "and if that doesn't work."

" Dad, he's not worth it. Come on, Max, let's get that eye cleaned up."

Scott made the mistake of reaching for Dorie. Lynne took him flat to his face and handed him to her deputies.

"Dorie?" Lynne said.

" I'm definitely pressing charges. He broke a restraining order, tried to kidnap my kids and attempted assault."

" I didn't .."

Scott didn't get his words out. The deputy who had him elbowed him square in the chest.

" Show some respect for the lady."

Jesse laughed.

" Now, Nate, that's going to have a talking to, of course, maybe it was that trick elbow, I asked you to have checked out."

Paul got up in Scott's face.

" I heard you like to beat up girls. Did you all know that?" Paul said to the deputies.

All eyes went to Dorie, who was

Now, playing the frail little lady.

Nate's grip got tighter.

"Ow."

A motorcycle roared up the drive, parked and came over.

Steve and Lisa came over to the group. Steve was Paul's friend and former co-worker when Paul was a Maine State trooper.

He saw the deputies and the guy in cuffs.

"Oh ho ho, what do we have here?"

Steve Lin was the nicest giant you ever wanted to mess with or his friends.

" Steve, this is Dorie's ex, you know, the one I told you beat her up." Paul knew Steve's mom was mentally abused by his father. Steve's whole body went ridge. Lisa grabbed Steve's arm.

" Steve, they have it under control. Don't ."

Under his girlfriend's grip, the tension went out of Steve's body. Lynne came over to Steve.

" Don't worry, my deputies got it.

We are going to enjoy the rest of this party, like that piece of crap never showed up. "

Lynne linked arms with Lisa and Steve and led them to the food table. Looking at the group, Lynne said.

" We worked too hard to let Scott ruin our day. Dorie, are you okay?"

" Yes, I'm fine, I would have loved to kick his ass, but I'll do that in court." Her kids came over to her and hugged her tight.

" It's okay, guys, Mama is fine."

Little Scott eyed his mother.

" Is daddy going to jail?"

" Oh, I certainly hope so."

The three kids said together.

" Good!"

Chapter 6

Everyone was having a great time, messy food, and festive fun on a bright sunny day. Paul pulled Lisa to the side. "Where's Oliver?"

"Most likely home pouting, which he has been doing a lot of lately. He really misses Benny."

"I told you to invite him."

"I did, Paul. I pleaded with him, and he said he'd just feel like an outsider."

"Outsider? You two are like family now; it's Benny's loss, but I think Oliver might have second thoughts if he knew what I knew."

" What do you know, old man?"

" That a certain handsome former special agent will be coming home later."

" What? Benny's coming home? Paul, he broke Oliver's heart. I don't know."

" Apparently, he couldn't think of anything else but Oliver. He quit, really quit, turned in his resignation weeks ago."

"What if Oliver won't have anything to do with him?"

" Well, then we have to find out. L say we go get our boy, Oliver, you say he's moping at home. Wanna take a ride?"

" Okay."

" Let me grab my keys."

" Paul, Steve left his keys in the bike."

" I knew there was something I liked about you."

As Paul peeled out, Steve, his mouth full of lasagna, threw up his arms."Hey!"

Oliver didn't live far from the Wiseman ranch. Paul and Lisa were there in little time.

" Do you think he'll come?"

" Come on, Lisa, hasn't Lin told you I have this way of talking that I usually get my way?"

" Actually, yes, putting it in nicer words than his... Paul can sell snow to Eskimos and manure to farmers."

Paul let out a huge belly laugh.

" Let's go get our boy."

Paul stood off to the side, Lisa rang the bell, and Oliver came to the door.

" Lisa? I thought you were at the BBQ?"

Paul stepped into view.

"She was, but she forgot the one thing I asked her nicely to bring."

" Paul."

" Don't Paul me, lock up and let's go."

" I won't feel comfortable without Benny. I don't fit in."

"What's wrong with you kids? You became part of my family, my flock, and when I invite you into my flock, you are flocked."

" No, No, no flocking today. I can't come. I'm not in the mood."

" Oh, you are flocking today. The whole family is waiting."

" Your family, Paul."

" Oliver, you are part of that family now. You don't have to be dating my son, I like you, I want you there. Hell, I even kidnapped Lin's girlfriend and stole his bike to come get you."

Oliver looked at Lisa, and she nodded.

"He's crazy. He goes around flocking everyone. He held me at gunpoint and told me to get on the bike, ranting about how he flocked you. I was scared, Oliver. Please come. He scares me."

"Fine, but don't expect me to have fun."

"Oh, you'll have fun. As head flocker, I'll make sure you have fun. "

Lisa couldn't hold it in anymore and burst out laughing.

" Come on, Oliver, we'll meet you there."

Lisa and Paul got back to the ranch. Steve was there, arms folded.

" Paul, stop stealing my stuff, and go find your own woman."

" I found her, remember? Besides, you didn't even leave your plate when we drove off."

Oliver drove up behind them in a beautifully restored 1969 champagne-colored Chevy Impala. Everyone came out to check out the car.

A lone figure stayed back in the back doorway, watching everything.

"Oliver!" Paul exclaimed, "What a beautiful car."

"Thanks, it was my grandfather's; his father gave it to him. He put it in a garage and never drove it. I found it, my dad said to take it. I restored it, frame up."

Jesse loved old cars.

" it's so cool. Would you ever sell it?"

" I dunno, Jesse, it's part of my family, then all the work I did on it."

Tiny and Moose started barking,

everyone was outside, and they were barking at something in the house. Everybody turned and looked toward the house. Paul said. " I'll go see what's going on."

He ran into the house.

" Tiny, Moose out," Paul yelled at them.

Paul came back out.

"What were they barking at dad?" Dorie looked at her father.

" There was a strange person in the house."

Jesse got up. " What?"

Paul left for him to sit back down. " Hey, Strange person, come on out."

Benny came through the screen door and did a little wave. His eyes went to Oliver, but Oliver just shook his head.

"Yeah, I can't do this. I'm going to get going. " Oliver was very upset.

Paul went over to Oliver.

" I'm sorry, I didn't realize.. "

Oliver scoffed. He was very tense.

" I feel set up. Maybe other people can deal with their ex's hanging around, but I can't. I gotta go."

Oliver got in the car and pulled out. Benny grabbed Lin's bike.

" Sorry, Steve, I'll bring it back."

Steve threw his hands up.

" Like father like son."

Benny followed Oliver. They got back to his house.

" Benny, I don't want you here."

" Ollie, I know you don't mean that. I know I hurt you badly. I panicked."

" You panicked?"

"Things started getting serious. I'm not good at serious. I'm so used to bouncing around the globe. When you started talking about marriage and kids, yeah I panicked. Ollie, I came back because I realized how much I need you in my life. I want you in my life... I love you."

Oliver let out a huge sigh. He loved Benny, too, but he didn't want someone who was going to go running at the first sign of a crisis.

" I don't know what to say, Benny. You hurt me. I blinked my eyes, and you were gone. What am I supposed to think now?"

" I know, and believe me, if I could go back in time, I'd change it. Ollie, you have to believe me, I'm done. I officially retired from police work."

Benny pulled papers from his back pocket. The papers were a signed copy of his resignation, Oliver glanced at them.

" That doesn't guarantee you won't take off again, Benny. How can I trust you?"

" I don't know, faith?"

" Faith?"

"Oliver, I can't keep saying I'm sorry, and I don't come with a guarantee. I just need you to trust me. Please come back to the party."

Oliver grabbed the second helmet. He got on the back of the bike, saying nothing more. He just sat there waiting.

Benny said to himself.

" Okay, it's a start."

When they got back to the party, Steve came over to the bike and took the keys.

" Crazy Wisemans "

Chapter 7

So the day was now half over. The backyard was looking good, ready for the bbq in two days.

Dorie was up to her elbows in dishes, and even tho everyone offered to help. She really needed a few minutes to clear her head. Scott, she thought to herself. How dare he? What was he thinking? Was he thinking at all? Yes, she'd fight tooth and nail for her kids, but they don't even want to be near Scott, and they have a genuine fear of him. A fear, so much, it made her wonder if he hit them.

There was a small knock at the door, a gentle tap. Dorie was shaken from her thoughts, jerking her head towards the door.

It was Max. He saw her reaction and held his hands up.

" I'm sorry. I just wanted to come see if you were okay."

" Yeah, I'm fine. I just needed to clear my head. I was just shocked. He showed up, you know. I thought we were done with him."

" I was going to punch his lights out, I'm not sure. I would have stopped if you hadn't pulled me off of him."

Dorie blushed. Considering she was a Grand Master in karate, it was nice for a man to stand up for her.

"That's sweet of you."

" Dorie, why did you stop coming to the stables with the kids? I loved it when you were around."

Dorie had no answer. She couldn't very well tell Max, she was jealous of Tammy.

" I just.."

" Tammy's my cousin, you know. I don't have any lady friend. I was so happy when you came around the stables cause I got to see you more. Now it's just when Paul or Jesse invite me up here."

" I saw you with Tammy. She was caressing your arm. I just thought, I don't know what I thought, but I couldn't bear to get hurt all over again. My divorce is still raw. Look what happened today. I'm sorry, Max, I couldn't come back to watch you with someone else."

"Tammy is touchy-feely. She cannot have a conversation without touching you. You should have asked me. I thought I did or said something wrong. Oh, Dorie, I am not Scott. I would never hurt you."

" I know, that's why I couldn't chance it. I didn't want to take that risk. I have so much to think about with the kids and how things would be if it didn't work out."

Max went to Dorie. The look he gave her was loving but intense. He caressed her cheek. All the worries left Dorie. She felt weak, putting her hand on Max's chest to steady herself. Max leaned into him to kiss her. Dorie's hand pulled him closer as she went on her tip toes. Their kiss was deep, like searching. Dorie felt safe, all her doubts draining from her body.

The giggles came from the doorway. Max and Dorie looked, three little munchkins giggling like crazy. Dorie shook her head.

"So much for secrecy. "

The kids spun toward the door.

" UNCLE JESSE, PAPA, WE GOT A SECRET."

They ran back out to the backyard. Dorie laid her head on Max's chest. Max kissed the top of her head.

" I know, this sounds crazy, Dorie,

but I have so many emotions lately. I think I'm falling in love."

" I'm sure we need a minute to figure this all out, but I feel so close to you. You are stealing my heart, Max. I never want this to end. To be honest, I think I'm falling in love with you hard."

Just then, Jesse comes through the door, imitating Ross on Friends.

" My sister, my best friend. My best friend and my sister. "

He pulled them into a group hug.

Dorie got swallowed up, pushing out of the embrace.

"Ok, I can't breathe, and you guys stink. Let's go get some fresh air.

The guys laughed, going to get cleaned up.

Dorie took a deep breath outside, trying to clear her head and reeling on what just happened. Scott, then Max, so many emotions. How dare Scott come here, demanding she let him see the kids. Alls she could remember was trying to get the kids to understand their father wasn't coming back. Trying to explain at their level, that he didn't want to be in their lives anymore. Their little searching eyes, but why, mama? Showing up today, what was Scott thinking? What was he thinking? Dorie meant what she said; she kept her license to practice law in Minnesota, and when she decided to stay in Maine, that was the first thing she did was apply to practice here. Funny how things work out. She is pressing charges against Scott.

" Hey, you okay?" Maddie touched Dorie's shoulder. Maddie is good for Jesse, compassionate, loving, smart and carefree. Her brother picked a good woman, Dorie thought to herself.

" Yes, I'm fine, shaken, but I'm okay. I just can't believe the balls on him. What did I see him him?"

" I don't know, Dorie. I'm guessing he wasn't always like this. "

" If I want to be honest, he was good, good with the kids too. Then, one day, it was like flipping a coin. He became this egotistical narcissist. I want to blame the job, but my father and brothers are all law enforcement, and it didn't change them."

"That's true. Let's get a cup of tea and just sit and chill out awhile. Calm down before going to bed."

" Thanks, Maddie, you're a good friend."

Chapter 8

Everyone had left. It had been a long day. It was hard for Max to leave Dorie. He wants to hold her tight and keep her safe. Scott was in jail, but there was still this atmosphere of apprehension: what if he made bail? What if he drove back and broke in? Okay, now I'm not leaving, Max thought to himself. He went to find Jesse.

" Hey, Jess." Max went to ask him if he could stay in one of the spare rooms.

" You know where blankets and towels are, and no, you never have to ask me if you can stay. You are always welcome here."

" Thanks, man."

" Don't forget, when Maddie got attacked, I moved myself into her place. I know how you feel.

Funny, I would never think Scott would turn out this way. He was a good guy once, but the way he lunged at Dorie earlier.. like rage."

" I wanted to rip his head off."

" Man, you don't tell the sheriff that." Both men laughed.

" Oh, right. Scratch that. "

Everyone went to bed. Jesse lay staring at the ceiling. He couldn't shake the feeling of something being wrong. Everyone was here. Steve and Lisa, Andy and Vee had gone home. But his family was here, and even Oliver stayed over. Oliver, Jesse never thought the day his little brother Benny would fall in love.

His cell went off, and Jesse jumped.

" Jess?" Maddy said groggily.

"It's the station, Mads. Go back to sleep" Jesse said to the already sleeping Maddy.

"Wiseman," Jesse listened. Ran his hand through his hair. Alls he wanted to do was get to Monday and celebrate the end of the summer with some messy food and fun.

" Are they sure it's him, Dougie? I mean … yeah, okay. No, no, I'll tell her. I'll be there in half an hour."

Jesse got dressed, going over the conversation with his senior deputy after Lynne. Murder.

He went to his father's room and tapped lightly. Paul came to the door and rubbed his eyes.

" Jess?"

" Dad, I need Lynne. Something came up." Lynne was already up and getting dressed.

" I had the most restless night," she said.

Jesse nodded ." Same here."

" What happened?" Paul looked anxious now.

Jesse told them about the conversation with Dougie.

"Sweet Lord," Paul said.

Jesse turned to Lynne.

" Come on, I guess they are already coming to get him."

" Where's everyone going?"

They all turned at once. Dorie looked so tiny in her pajamas.

" Umm, Lynne and I, we got called in."

" What happened? " Dorie looked at their faces. Seeing the anxious looks on her family's faces. " What did Scott do, now?"

" Dorie, we really have to go. We can talk later."

Jesse and Lynne left.

" Dad?"

Paul took a deep breath and looked at his daughter... She looked about 12.

"Dorie, they are going in to find out something about Scott."

Dorie waited for a beat.

" Dad, I'm an adult, please.."

" Scott is a wanted felon, Dorie. He has been on the lam for weeks."

" Felon?" Dorie searched her father's face.

" He was in a bar fight, and it kept going out in the parking lot,

Scott shot the guy and just left him there. He bled to death. Scott murdered him, Dorie. "

Dorie turned pale; her words escaped her, and then she fainted. Paul caught her, picked her up and carried her to the sofa.

Then Paul sat down and prayed.

It took Dorie a while to come around; everyone was concerned that she had gone into shock. Max was pacing back and forth, not knowing what to do. Paul told him to sit.

" She's a strong woman, Max. I think she definitely will be okay." Dorie then reached out her hands. Max kneeled on the floor in front of her and took them.

" Dorie, please be okay."

"Max? Oh, Max, I had the strangest dream that they told me Scott murdered someone. Just imagine that. Scott?"

Max looked at Paul.

"Dorie, honey," Paul's voice wavered.

"Dad? It was a dream, right? The father of my children isn't some killer. I mean Scott is a lot of things but he wouldn't kill someone." Tears burned Dorie's eyes.

" I'm sorry, honey, it's true."

Dorie took a huge breath and let out a cry."

" Mommy!" The kids were calling for her. Paul went to comfort them. Dorie sat up and Max sat next to her, saying nothing but holding her hands.

They sat waiting,Jesse was supposed to call with an update.

The kids settled down and Paul came back out to sit with them.

The three of them sat in silence, almost like they were afraid to speak and miss Jesse's call.

When the phone finally rang, it was Paul's cel, Paul answered, listening intently. Nodding.

" Okay, son, see you when you get home."

Maddie had come out of the kitchen, she had been putting stuff away, trying to give Dorie and Max some privacy.

" So authorities from Alaska picked him up and he's gone. Scott has some pretty serious charges against him. If he gets convicted. He may never see the outside of prison again. I'm sorry, honey."

Dorie just sat, shell shocked, no words came. Turning into Max's shoulder, she sobbed quietly.

Everyone was quiet after, Jesse called. Maddie and Paul had come back, into the parlor, They sat on the couch opposite of Dorie and Max.

" Dad, how could this happen,

Where did Scott go, and where did this monster come from.. how do I explain to my kids."

A loud shuddering sob came from Dorie, Max held her closer, she was shivering..

" Look Dorie, I talked to a few guys back in Minnesota, Scott didn't handle power well. His narcissistic behavior turned everyone against each other, when reviews came around, nobody would sign off, the Chief got involved. They let Scott go, this wasn't long after you left, from what I heard, he opened and closed the bars every night."

Chapter 9

Vee noticed something off with Andy all day since he showed up at the Wiseman's. When she asked him if everything was okay, he looked like a frightened deer.

When they got in the car to leave the Wiseman's ranch, she said to him.

"Andy, what's going on? Did something happen at work?"

" Work?"

"Yeah, you know that place, you sit at the counter with Ray, playing rummy, til someone comes in and buys one of your overpriced antiques."

Andy laughed. Andy laughed too hard.

" I'm fine, Vee. Ray left early, I had a last-minute customer and closed up a little later."

" Andy, look you don't have to tell me anything, you don't want to but don't lie or, more like leave things out. That answer was so full of holes. Swiss cheese would be jealous, okay?"

" What?"

" Something tells me what you just said and what you're not saying is what's bothering you."

"Everything is fine, okay, really."

"Sure, can you drop me off, at home?"

"I thought you were staying with me…"

"Yeah, well, I'm thinking there is really only one reason, you would be, not telling me, what's wrong. Maybe you found someone else, which (tears came as Vee's words got lost in her throat) is fine. I don't own you."

Andy felt like the biggest jerk, he pulled the car over, Vee went for the door handle.

"No, no Vee stop, stop..please, that's not it at all."

Vee sulked back in the seat, pouting, she was so beautiful.

"Can we go home?"

Vee threw him a look like, you wish. "No."

"My ex-girlfriend came into the shop."

" Yeah? That's it?"

" Looking for me, wanting to try it again."

"You want to?"

" No, no, and I told her that, but Vee, I don't trust her. The last thing, I wanted is you getting hurt, in her little games."

" Hurt?"

"Stella, when we first got together, sophomore year,she was sweet and innocent, just a good kid. By junior year, does the movie Mean Girls mean anything to you? I was the star of the hockey team, so she thought that others were beneath her and her little clique."

"So you think she's going to hurt me because…. ?"

" Stella is used to getting her way, right now, she sees you as an obstacle. I love you, Vee. You should know that by now. I told her as much. "

" So what did she do? Leave."

"Yeah, she left, bought $3,000 worth of antique toys, told me to throw them out, and left."

" $3,000? Throw them out?"

"You know, to show me, she's loaded."

Vee laughed.

" Come on." Vee looked at Andy.

" That's the whole truth."

"Hmmmm."

"What?"

" Maybe she's looking for a girlfriend! " Andy laughed.

" Are you coming home with me, miss Smarty pants."

" Oh Fine I suppose, and don't do that anymore, no secrets."

" No secrets."

Chapter 10

Benny and Oliver finished eating breakfast, Oliver just looked at Benny.

" I don't get it, you're a cop, where did you learn how to cook?" Benny laughed at the confusion on his boyfriend's face.

" Ex-federal agent, My mother made us all take turns cooking, Jesse and Dorie are amazing cooks, too. So is my father, I guess, it's from being raised in a family, that tried to keep it together when most families were falling apart."

" I get that, my dad thinks it's sissy for men to cook or clean. Women's work, he'd say."

Benny did a couple of bodybuilder poses.

" Do I look sissy to you?"

" I'd hate to tell you, Yes!"

" Hey!" Benny playfully nudged Ollie.

" My father thinks being gay makes us feminine.. which in his eyes is sissy."

" Wait til he meets me.. he'd have to change his mind."

" Benny, my father never changes his mind.. he's so living in the past, it's like 1950 in my parents' house."

" What does your mother think?"

" She doesn't, she loves my father, so she takes everything with a grain of salt. Patience of a saint."

"Will your father have a problem with me?"

"No, no Benny, he's a lot of things, but my dad has accepted my lifestyle completely.. when I came out to my parents, they said they already knew, and that could never change their love for me."

" What about your sister?"

" Carolyne?, what can I say? My sister is my sister. Carolyne rolls to the beat of her own drummer.

She dates this rich dude, so she looks down on people."

" Let's take a ride."

" Where are we going?"

"You'll see."

Benny drove a little bit and pulled up in front of an old fashion building being used as offices.

"We are here."

"Where's here?" Oliver was trying to get a better look.

" I'm going to open a law office and call Poland home. I thought about staying with Jess, but it's a bit crowded there. I guess I'll rent an apartment. "

Benny looked at Oliver to see if he could see what he was thinking. But Oliver was quiet.

" What are you thinking, Honey?"

" Law office?"

" Yeah, I figured it might help Dorie too. She could work out of the office or at home."

" Benny, you're going to sit behind a desk for 8 hours?"

" I have a law degree. It's something I can do."

" You also have muscles, so you could become a professional wrestler."

Benny looked hurt.

"Oh, Benny, I'm sorry."

" I thought you'd be happy. I'm trying to settle down. I wanted to be with you."

" You want to be with me, and you're going to rent an apartment when I own a house?"

" I didn't want to just assume…"

" Assume what, that I love you and want you to move in? You are throwing yourself into a career. I could almost bet, you will be miserable. What about the Maine police, like your dad?"

" Truthfully, I don't want to be a cop or agent or go through law files. You are right, but I studied law and its income."

" But you will be miserable."

"I'll be here with you. I won't be miserable. I need something to do. I could afford to retire and sit at home. My last pay afforded me that with smart investments and my savings, I'm set. I can't sit around twiddling my thumbs ."

" You need to do something more that you are dealing with people.. not just clients, real human relations. Don't jump from one extreme to the next.

What about a fitness club? A personal trainer gym, aerobic studio." Oliver was looking past Benny to the future.

" I'll think about it, Thanks Oliver."

Oliver put his hand on Benny's forearm.

"When you're ready, we can talk about you moving in. Even if you want your own space, there's a studio downstairs. I'm not ready to give you up. I really do love and care about your crazy ass."

Sitting in the car.

Benny was quiet. Oliver knew there was something more, good or bad, he needed to know.

" Okay, Benny, what are you not saying?"

Benny blew out a breath.

" Oh, now I can't wait to hear."

" It's not bad, it's just I know you hate me doing jobs with risk."

" Risk?"

" Volunteer job. I signed up to be a volunteer fireman."

Oliver turned to look at Benny, a little confused.

" BENNY! Why would I be upset about that? "

" You hated me being a federal agent because of the risk. Firemen risk their lives, too."

" I know that I'm usually there with them, but Benny, fighting a fire, yes risky.. having a shootout out with a drug lord and his AR-15. Really?"

" So you're not upset?"

" I'm not upset at all. Benny, I have to tell you though, you cannot give up everything in your life to make me happy. Relationships are a compromise.

You will resent me after a while, feeling that I always get my way, I don't want that. Yes, it scared me about you being undercover in South America. I actually think it's wonderful if you become a fireman. Even full-time. It's a job to fill your passion for helping people."

" You think I should be a full-time firefighter?"

" I think you, should stop worrying about what I want, and just be yourself. Our relationship needs honesty. Do you honestly want to do 60-80 hours a week in a law office? Come on, Benny, really?"

Benny threw Oliver a side look.

" You know, I love you, Benny, but forcing things, pretending, it doesn't help. "

" I know. I love you too, so I can go talk to the chief tomorrow?"

" I'll go with you if you want. "

" No, I'll be okay. I'm a big boy."

Oliver laughed.

Oliver started the car, heading for home, he realized his love for Benny grew threefold tonight. The boy has my heart, Oliver smiled to himself.

Chapter 11

Dorie was doing dishes. Jesse had a dishwasher, but doing dishes actually calmed Dorie's nerves. Dorie started crying, deep, heavy sobs. How did we get to this spot, she thought to herself. My children, my poor kids, their father is going to jail for a long long time.

" You okay, Sis? "

Dorie turned into Jesse's shoulder, crying even harder.

" Hey, hey Dorie, look at me. It's going to be okay."

"Everything is so messed up, Jesse. Where do me and the kids go from here?"

" What are you talking about Dor? You have a family that loves you and the kids, a guy that is wild about you. Aside from all that, remember what mom and dad always said about life.

"You can only live it 24 hours at a time."

Jesse lowered his forehead to Dorie's.

" The most important thing is, he can never hurt you or the kids again."

Maddie came into the kitchen.

" What's going on?"

" Dorie is a little down, she feels lost and worried about the kids."

"Dorie, Scott made his bed, has to sleep in it. We will get through this together.."

Dorie nodded "thank you "

Paul came into the kitchen, "Okay folks, time to put our happy faces on, guest are arriving."

"Jesse, grab the ribs and hot dogs and hamburgers. Paul yelled up the stairs " SCOTTY, KATIE, NOAH, let's go. You guys are buns, plates and cups. Dorie

You got salads, potato, macaroni, green. Maddie pickles, olives, onions, condiments and salad dressings.

Lynne, the refreshments and chips, please.

I'm going to greet the guest."

Paul went over to Maddie, he leaned into whisper in her ear.

" You left something in the bathroom waste basket."

He passed her a small box, and smiled.

Maddie looked a little surprised but nodded.

Paul nodded back.

Maddie laughed.

"What are you laughing at?" Paul was confused by his son's fiancée. Was she embarrassed?

"Paul, what made you think this was mine?"

" Maddie, there's nothing to be embarrassed about being pregnant."

" Paul, I'm not embarrassed because it's not my test."

" What? I mean, I just assumed...

Dorie? No, right? Maybe Vee took it here so Andy would see it?"

" Paul, Vee did not take a pregnancy test in someone else's house."

" Not you, I can't image Dorie, not Vee.. I mean, who... "

Suddenly, the light bulb went on over Paul's head. He looked at Maddie like a deer caught in headlights..bing bing bing.

" No, come on, that's crazy."

" Why is it crazy she is still childbearing age?"

Paul scoffed.

" My kids are all grown, I have grandchildren."

" There's no rules, Paul."

" I need to help Jesse with the bbq."

"Right."

Paul went outside to the grill.

One look at his father, who looked pale, Jesse knew something was wrong. Jesse grabbed his father's arm.

"Dad, what's wrong? Are you okay? Do I have to call 911?"

Jumpy, something Paul never was. " What?" Paul looked at Jesse like he just arrived from Mars.

" Dad, do you need to sit down?"

" What, Jess? No, I'm fine, I'll be okay. Maybe a little crazy about the BBQ, you know what I mean?" Jesse knew Paul was

lying to him, though he now realized his father wasn't sick, he was worried.

Benny and Oliver showed up, and Andy and Vee.

The guests were arriving, lots and lots of them. All in white, white tee shirts, white tank tops, white summer dresses, even white halter tops all looking to get messy with the Wiseman's yummy food.

"Dad." Benny put his hand on Paul's shoulder. Paul winced and turned toward his son.

" Benny?"

" Did I just hurt you?"

" No, no, you surprised me."

Benny and Jesse looked at each other and then back at Paul.

"I just wanted to ask you how everything was going?"

" Going? Everything is fine. Just wonderful."

His sons didn't believe Paul for one second.

Benny got Jesse on the side.

" What's going on with dad? "

" I don't know, Benny, he was so pale earlier, he scared the crap out of me."

" Should we take him to hospital?"

" No, I don't think it's medical; something is bothering him. Let's ask Dorie."

So Jesse and Benny asked Oliver to man the grill with Paul.

"Oh boy! Yes!"

The Wiseman boys headed for the kitchen.

Dorie just pulled outa tray of potato salad and looked at her brothers.

" What's wrong?"

Jesse spoke first.

"Did something happen with Dad?

"What do you mean? What's wrong with him?"

" He's acting strange, jumpy and kinda worried."

Dorie shook her head. "He hasn't said anything to me."

Maddie came into the kitchen. Jesse asked her.

" Mads, Dad, talk to you today. He's acting kind of strange."

Oh no, Maddie thought, it's really not my place to say anything.

" He told me to get pickles and ketchup."

Everyone laughed.

Lynne came into the kitchen, and Benny asked her.

" Lynne, anything up with dad?"

"What do you mean?"

" He's just not himself."

" Well, let's go see what's bothering him."

The whole gang went out to talk to Paul, and Andy and Vee joined, too. Paul saw them heading toward him, and his stomach did a somersault.

Dorie got to her father first.

" Daddy, are you feeling alright?"

" Yeah, baby girl. I'm just fine."

Paul looked at Lynne, and just like that, Lynne knew what was bothering Paul. Lynne laughed.

Everyone looked at her.

" You found the test, didn't you, Paul?"

Now, everyone looked confused.

Jesse blurted out.

" What test?"

" My pregnancy test, I wasn't thinking and left it in the waste basket."

The three Wiseman kids looked at their father. Lynne caught Paul's eyes.

" Surprise, I'm pregnant."

Paul froze, which upset Lynne, and she walked back into the house. Maddie and Vee went after her.

Dorie looked at her father.

" Dad, go after her."

" I don't know what to say."

" When you start talking, it will come to you, but she needs you to come after her. Now go."

Paul went into the house.

Maddie and Vee left Paul and Lynne alone. Paul sat down on the couch next to Lynne. He let out a huge breath.

" Lynnie "

" You don't have to be involved, Paul. We can go our separate ways. I'll raise the baby on my own."

Paul looked stunned.

" You think I'd do that? I love you, Lynne. I'm just shocked. My last kid was born 27 years ago. I'm sorry if I hurt your feelings. I couldn't process, I just froze."

"So you don't mind having a baby with me? Lynne sniffed and wiped tears.

" Mind? That baby is a product of our love, honey. I'm 58 years old . I thought my baby-making days were over. You are giving me a gift."

Paul grabbed her hand.

" Okay, back to bbq!"

Lynne laughed.

When Paul got outside, Steve Lin and Lisa were out there.

" Hey Steve, Lisa, congratulate me. I'm gonna be a daddy again."

" What now? " Steve laughed.

The ladies went to Lynne, and the guys all shook Paul's hand.

Chapter 12

Things were looking better. The party was in full swing everyone was having a great time. Eating, talking, playing games, and someone with a fiddle started a square dance. After the last do si do, Andy and Vee headed for

some food. Someone kept bumping into Andy. He turned and went to say something. The person spoke first.

"Andy, image seeing you here."

Stella's voice dripped with sarcasm.

Vee looked at Andy for some kind of explanation but only saw daggers aimed at this woman. Andy grabbed Vee's hand and headed for the house.

The first person they saw was Benny.

" Benny, can you tell your dad something came up, and Vee and I had to head out."

Vee grabbed Andy's arm.

"Andy, what's going on? I don't want to leave."

"Babe, that was Stella, and she's going to go after you. I know it."

Benny jumped in. " Who's Stella?"

They both looked at him.

"Andy, I don't care. I'm not leaving. I'm having a good time."

" Vee," Andy sighed.

" Don't Vee me, I'm not giving this woman the satisfaction of us leaving. I'm definitely not afraid of her. How did she even get in?"

"I don't know, good question"

Benny had to know. " Who's Stella?"

"His ex. Gosh, Benny, keep up."

This made Andy laugh.

"Are you sure, Vee?"

" Look, Andy, what can she do, call me poor and ugly? Come on.

I'm starving. I didn't wait all this time to miss eating."

Andy smiled. It's why he loved Vee. She was real, as they come.

Andy knew Stella, though, and it didn't take long. He and Vee were in line for food. Vee got to Jesse and the ribs, and someone bumped into her.

" Clumsy cow, watch where you're going," Stella said snobby-like.

Jesse just put some ribs on Vee's plate. Vee pretended she was startled and fell forward, landing her plate right on Stella's chest and a forearm to her face.

" Oh my gosh, I'm such a clumsy cow," Vee said sarcastically.

Stella tried to stand, but Vee was standing on her hair.

Vee squatted down.

" You need to stay away from my guy, or I will show you how real Maine girls take care of people like you. Oh yeah, I'd suggest you leave."

Andy and Jesse just stood there, looking at each other, mouths open. Vee got off of Stella's hair.

Stella went to say something, but her friend grabbed her and pulled her to the back gate.

Andy and Jesse started to chant.

" Vee Vee Vee !"

Vee laughed.

" Jesse, I need another plate of ribs, I really am starving!"

Everyone laughed.

Andy and Vee sat at one of the tables. Joined by Paul and Lynne, Lynne reached out the Vee.

" You okay?"

" Me?" Vee looked surprised.

" Yeah, tough as you are, girl, that was an embarrassing situation she put you in."

" I'm fine, Lynne, really. I suppose that. She might come after me again."

" She will count on it," Andy added.

Paul just shook his head. "Is it me or has the whole world gone crazy."

Benny and Oliver sat down too.

" I loved when Vee was standing on her hair, and she was trying to get up." Benny said, laughing a whooping belly laugh.

They all started laughing. Maddie came over.

" Ok, children, as much as I loved Vee's forearm to the face.

The children are very impressed. I don't want them to think violence is the answer. Although with people like her, I'm guessing an added uppercut was justified."

Everyone stared at Maddie for a moment. Then broke out laughing.

"Guys, I'm serious," Maddie said, laughing.

Which only made this crazy group laugh harder, now, everyone in the yard was staring at them. Vee stood up and addressed the guest.

" They are laughing at me, folks. I apologize for making that scene earlier. Please continue to eat this wonderful food, and have fun.

Everyone clapped, and little Noah came over and hugged Vee around her waist. Vee kneeled down and gave him a big hug and kiss. Dorie turned to Andy.

" Looks like you got competition."

Vee sat back down next to Andy, a little misty-eyed.

"Andy, I want one of them."

"I don't know, Vee, I don't think Dorie wants to sell any of them."

Vee swatted Andy on the shoulder. He couldn't believe how much he loved this woman.

" I loved you, Vee." he kissed her on the forehead.

Jesse, who seemed a little emotional.

"Okay, you two, break it up, baby making is not allowed at this gathering. It's not listed as one of the games cause I would have an unfair advantage." everyone laughed, Jesse said to Andy and Vee.

" Don't make me separate, you two."

Paul grabbed Lynne's hand.

" I love you, Lynnie."

" Even pregnant?"

" Of course, don't be crazy. I was just taken a little off guard. Like I said, I haven't had a baby around since Ben. that's a long time."

" I thought you'd be upset because I'm not Jessica."

" What? Oh, Lynne, stop that. I made my peace with all that. You are going to be my wife. Jessica was my wife. I'll always love her, but you, you and this baby are my life."

Max showed up with Tammy. They headed over to the table. Max looked at Dorie and gave a sexy smile.

" So what are we talking about?" Max is looking at everyone.

Jesse is not missing a beat.

"Baby-making competition, you in?"

" Come again?"

Maddie jabbed Jesse with an elbow, but Jesse kept going.

"Baby-making competition, I mean, you do know how babies are made, right?"

" I owe you, Jess. I will get you back, I promise."

" I'll be waiting, my friend. I'll be waiting."

Dorie went over to Max and gave him a sweet kiss. This time, Benny couldn't resist.

" Hey, you two, no baby-making in the dining area. People are eating."

Dorie flipped Ben the bird.

Benny acted shocked.

" Children, don't make me get the belt " Paul laughed.

53

Chapter 13

The BBQ was going great, with a few bumps in the day. Someone tried to sneak liquor in, one of Paul's pet peeves. He had no problem with people drinking at home with their kids, but at a gathering with other people's children, he just didn't like it.

With the amount of people that show up at these BBQs, having liquor around was an invitation for trouble. Hell, people did not even need liquor to get in trouble, Paul thought to himself.

Even so, things went great. Dorie outdid herself on the dessert.. she made a lava cake, shaped like a volcano as big as a wedding cake. The kids were all going nuts over it.

" My mom made it! " Paul heard Scotty bragging to Lauren and Laney, Edna's twin granddaughters, " Our mom," Katie corrected him. " my mom, too." Little Noah piped in. Everyone laughed.

Lynne's nephew David, who had been away with his parents, went over to Dorie and gave her a big hug.

" I love volcanoes!"

Edna's grandsons Colt and Luke cheered, too.

Seems Dorie's cake was a huge hit with the kids.

After the cake was served, people started leaving.

Only the bonfire was left. Jesse was kind of glad there were fewer people around for that, especially the people with children. Tired kids get reckless.

Dorie's kids and a couple of others went into the house to watch a Disney movie.

The night was beautiful, the fire everyone huddled together.

Someone put on some music, on their phone.

A door slammed, and a car roared off. Everyone looked in the direction of the house.

Benny came out, he looked at his family and friends. He shook his head.

" I don't want to talk about it."

Oliver wasn't with him.

Lisa, Oliver's paramedic partner and best friend, let out a sigh. She knew Oliver could be difficult but thought Benny was good for him. Her boyfriend, Steve, gave her hand a little squeeze.

In most families, everyone would be complaining about clean up, at the Wiseman ranch, they made little games out of the clean up. Who collected the most cups or plates? Who folded the most tablecloths? The only job nobody wanted was cleaning the grills. It usually fell on Jesse to do them. But he could hardly complain. Cleaning the grills actually relaxed him. As Dorie says, doing dishes relaxes her. Jesse worried about Benny, he knew his brother and he had a feeling Benny was done with Oliver. After scrubbing the grills clean, Jesse went and sat down with Benny, a minute later, Dorie sat on the other side of Benny. None of them said a word. They didn't have to, always being so close, they knew when to talk and when to keep quiet.

Maddie and Max joined the siblings just sitting there.

Around 10 pm, the last of the guests started to leave, all the goodbyes were said, and now it was just family. Benny still didn't say anything, and nobody asked.

Paul had been playing horseshoes with Lynne. They came over, and Paul squeezed Benny's shoulder as he went past him and ruffled his hair like he was five.

" I think everyone had a good time." Paul said. " especially Vee." Everyone laughed. Andy and Vee had left a little while ago. Andy wasn't feeling well.. blaming Jesse's ribs, at first, then said his diabetes was making him a little light-headed.

By 11 pm, everyone was ready for bed.

Everyone said their good nights.

Nobody saw Max slip into Dorie's room, and nobody would see him slip out before dawn to head to the stables.

Chapter 14

"Morning" Lynne came into the kitchen. Maddie and Dorie were having coffee.

"Morning Lynne, coffee?" Dorie went to the coffee pot.

" Yes, please, before all that morning sickness hits."

" I definitely don't miss that "

Dorie said as she poured coffee.

"How are things going with you and Max, Dorie? I missed him leaving last night. Did he leave early?" Maddie asked.

David, Lynne's nephew, came in followed by Scott, Katie and Noah. Dorie was never so happy to see her kids, to avoid Maddie's question.

Dorie got the bowls, milk and spoons, the big box of cereal.

Paul and Benny getting up and coming in the kitchen. Dorie got two more cups of coffee.

" So what are we doing today?" Paul asked Lynne.

Lynne took this week off, take David's school clothes shopping.

" We are going to the mall." Lynne said as excitedly as she could manage. All the kids cheered. Paul teased.

"Oh, you guys are coming too?"

The kids all giggled.

Paul looked at Benny.

" Ben, you want to come? I'll buy you an ice cream."

" I don't know, Dad."

Lynne looked at Benny.

"Come on, Benny, it'll be fun."

Benny nodded.

"Dorie? Maddie?" Paul said.

Maddie smiled.

" I'm in."

Dorie looked at her kids, pleading eyes.

" How will we all fit?"

" We will," Paul said.

" Okay, fine, as long as me and Maddie get to go in one store we like."

Maddie said, " I'm looking for a birthday gift for Jesse. Poor thing, I got called in at 2 am. Maybe we can drop in on Jackie at Skipper's and get Jesse some lunch on the way home."

The others didn't really know Jackie, Maddie's friend Jimmy's fiancée, but agreed to lunch.

Shopping was fun. The kids all got new outfits, shoes, and school supplies.

Maddie found Jesse, a model car he'd been dying to do.

Paul and Benny got some fishing supplies.

Lynne dragged Paul over to a maternity store. She didn't buy anything, yet but wanted to check stuff out.

" Lynne, honey. Don't you think this is pushing the clock?"

" No, I mean, it's going to happen. I just wanted to see my options."

" Okay."

" Paul, are you sure you are okay? You know, my whole being pregnant."

" Okay? What do you mean?"

" Well, you exactly expecting to be a dad at 58, were you?"

" Truthfully, no, and I told you it caught me off guard. Look, Lynne, get that thought out of your head. I love you, and we are having a baby. In today's society, 9 out of 10 kids are raised by their grandparents. How would it be much different."

Lynne thought about it for a minute, but Paul did make sense.

Maybe it's me, Lynne thought to herself. I don't want anyone saying your grandchild is adorable. She didn't let things roll off her back as easily as Paul.

" I guess it's not."

Paul took Lynne's hand, squeezed it, and gave her a quick peck on the cheek.

" I love you," Paul whispered in her ear.

" I love you, too."

Chapter 15

Benny got home, he told everyone he was going to lay down to rest his eyes.

"I'm fine, just a bit of a headache. I'll live."

Paul, Jesse, and Dorie exchanged looks; they knew better. Benny the wild child, as much as he tried to hide it, he was hurting.

" Go on, Benny, go rest, we are going to get cleaned up and help get a light supper together."

Paul told his son, it made him miserable to see his son this way.

Jesse the comic, " Do you want me to tuck you in?"

Benny laughed. " You are a real jerk, you know that Jess?"

"Makes me a better sheriff, brother." Jesse smiled at his little brother while gesturing him to go on.

Benny got in his room, pulled his shirt off, flinging in the direction, of the small hamper in his room.

Well, Benny alone again, he thought to himself. Plopping himself on the bed. Thinking about Oliver was useless. Meeting in July, broke up in August, and got back together in September.. Oliver wanted to get married, he insisted they get married. Benny was caught off guard that the conversation was even brought up, he did know he loved Oliver, but the marriage wasn't even on his radar. He hadn't told anyone, but Benny had fell in love with a woman in South America, it was mostly sexual, but he developed feelings for her, he could have very well told her he loved her, but he didn't.

Never having feelings for a woman before, Benny convinced himself it was a one-time thing and the relationship wouldn't last because he liked men.

I couldn't marry Oliver, and Benny kept going over it in his head. I just don't think he's my forever after. I like living in the moment, with no five-year plans, and no day planners. I'm Benny Wiseman, and I'm just here for today.

He started thinking about Ana,

how she made him come alive, how she cried when Benny told her, he had to leave. Old feelings stirred inside him, it was possible this was why Benny couldn't commit to Oliver, at first he thought Oliver was his soulmate, but more and more, they showed their differences.

There was a knock at the door.

"Yeah?" Benny wasn't in the mood for company or talking, he just wanted to lay here, not thinking.

Jesse opened the door and stuck his head in.

" I'm only here 'cause I was told to come talk to you, I can stand here, pretend to talk to you. I know you don't want to tell me about your feelings."

Benny laughed.

"Oh, Jesse, you are right. I don't want to talk or think or anything."

" That bad?"

"About Oliver? No. It would have happened eventually. Life.. I will tell you, but not today. Thank you."

" Benny, I'm always here for you."

" I know"

Jesse left.

Benny closed his eyes and started doing deep breathing, it didn't stop his mind from racing. I feel like a pinball machine, a little silver ball bouncing off the corners of my mind.

I quit my job. I broke up with Oliver. I moved in with Jesse. I applied to the Maine Fire Department all in one month.

I quit my job. Benny lulled into a deep sleep, his woke him up.

A groggy "Hello."

"Benny Wiseman?"

" Yes."

" Benny, this is Chief Ryan of Maine Fire Department, are you still interested in joining the MFD?"

" Yessir"

" Well, why don't you stop down the firehouse? You'll be going through the academy, but I'd like to meet you. I know you were a special agent, I'm guessing you have the fitness part down unless you gained a 100 lbs last month. So will I see you tomorrow? "

" Yessir"

" Great! Welcome to Station 4, Benny, see you tomorrow."

The Chief hung up.

Benny blinked.. and just like that, he was going to be a firefighter.

Chapter 16

"A firefighter?" Jesse said like it was some kind of disease.

" Benny? You're a cop, not a firefighter; firefighters run into burning buildings." Paul looked confused.

" Are you sure about this Benny?

I thought you were going to do something easy like stop speeding trains. " Dorie wanted her brother to open the law office, not for her but he had a safe career.

" It's not something I jumped into, I've been thinking about it for a while."Benny knew his family would worry, but not this bad.

Lynne didn't understand her future husband and his family. Benny walked gang ridden streets, he ran toward bullets not fire, he was level-headed and knew what he wanted.

"Why are you all against this?" She said.

The four Wiseman's looked at her, three like she appeared from a far distant planet, one

with a smile and respect.

" He's done more dangerous stuff. He's smart and brave. I'm proud of him."

Benny stood up and went over and hugged his future stepmom.

" Thanks, Lynne, not if you'll excuse me, I have to go meet my new boss."

" Benny, we are proud of you too, but if you get hurt, I'm gonna kick your ass." Dorie meant it.

Paul and Jesse agreed.

Benny left, off to his new future.

Benny got to the fire station. He didn't know what to expect. One of the men came over to him.

" Can I help you?"

" I'm looking for Chief Ryan."

" Are you the new probie?"

"I'm hoping so. I have to go through training. I'm Benny."

"Victor, call me Vic. The Chief is in his office. Come on. Don't worry about training. You look fitter than 90 % of this house."

Vic said, laughing, as he led the way back.

Benny liked Vic. If that was any indication of how the people of this house were, he'd like it here.

Vic knocked on the Chief's door,

Chief Ryan looked up from his computer.

" Wiseman, you made it! You met Vic. He's the heart of Station 4, best lieutenant I ever had."

Then the alarm went off, and Benny figured the meet and greet was over.

" How about riding along, Wiseman? See what you'll be doing in live action."

" Yeah, sure."

The other firefighters were a great group. Benny wasn't sure if Station 4 would be where he would wind up, but he wouldn't complain.

The fire was just a dumpster fire, with some kids playing around. The mood in the truck was very serious, business-like, and professional. Benny was happy about that, not much for small talk with strangers. When they got back to the station, that they called their " house", the mood lightened to almost playful.

" Hey Doggie, where's the grub?"

A tall blond man responded

" In the fridge, you cooking?"

"Oh come on, we want to live."

A pretty brunette named Cheryl,

Complained.

Benny took it all in. He wanted to want this, the public service, the risk of helping others, the playful coworkers, he really did. In the end, tho, Benny knew in his heart he wasn't a firefighter. I'm a cop. Looking across the street at the police station, Benny started to walking towards the building but stopped himself. I need to think this out, he thought to himself, I just can't keep jumping around. Benny got in his car. Tomorrow is another day.

Chapter 17

Vee had been up, showered, made breakfast and gotten ready to go to the shop. Andy was still in bed, which was weird because he was a morning person. Vee went into the bedroom and sat on the bed.

" Hey, sleepy head, Ray's gonna worry that you're not there before him."

Andy didn't answer her.

" Andy ?"

Vee shook Andy hard a couple of times before he responded. Looking up at her, Andy was out of focus.

" Vee?"

" Andy, what's the matter?"

"I think I'm just going to stay in bed today. I'm really tired."

Vee wasn't sure what to do. Andy really looked terrible. She called the shop and told them she wouldn't be in today. Then Vee called Ray, telling him Andy wasn't feeling well.

" He wasn't looking to hot all weekend, then that damn girl showed up. I think stress is upsetting him and maybe setting his diabetes off."

That did make sense, Vee thought. Hanging up with Ray, who told Vee to maybe take Andy to a hospital or atleast call his doctor.

Andy groaned. Vee went to him after calling his name a couple of times.

" Andy, Andy"

She manually opened his eyes. They were rolled back in his head. She dialed 911, then she dialed Jesse. Telling Jesse what was happening, she heard him curse in the background.

" Vee, I'll be there in a few minutes. Sounds like Diabetic coma, just keep trying to talk to him."

That's what she did.

" Andy, Andy, come on, wake up."

Then, after a couple of minutes, she was frightened and frustrated. Vee snapped

"Don't you dare leave me now, Andy Levesque, don't you dare."

Then she heard the sirens.

" Oh, thank God. Hang in there, Andy. Help is here. I love you, and please be okay."

The paramedics could see Andy was in a diabetic coma. They administered Glucagon, it took a few minutes but Andy came out of it, real groggy.

" Vee?" He reached out.

Vee took his hand, trying not to get in the way of the medics.

"Andy, you're going to be okay."

" Mam, we are taking him in. Will you follow us."

Jesse came in the room, he had been waiting outside, not wanting to get in the way.

"Come on, Vee. I'll take you.

In the car, Vee cried all the way.

" Vee, Andy's going to be okay, they'll adjust his meds, keep him a couple of days for observation, and he'll get some rest. Andy probably got a little too stressed out, this week, everything that happened at the BBQ, you know"

" I was so scared Jesse, I thought Andy was going to die, I just…
I love him, so much, I could imagine him not being here."

" Well, you don't have to worry about that.. Andy is one tough
SOB, trust me, he'll fight anything thrown at him."

Jesse looked over at Vee, she looked all of 15, her eyes were
shiny, nose and cheeks swollen, she was beautiful. Andy was a lucky
guy.

" All right, let's get to the hospital."

Jesse put the siren on and floored it, getting in front of the
ambulance for an escort.

Vee was so quiet in the passenger seat of Jesse's car he saw the
tears slip down her eyes. Jesse reached out to take her hand. She then
quietly sobbed, trying so hard to be brave.

" Vee, he's gonna be okay, he came around. That's a good sign."

"This time, Jesse, he came around this time. I hate this disease.
It doesn't matter if you do everything right.. he does everything right.
Eats right, exercises, and checks his blood glucose twice a day. He
does everything right, " Vee finally broke. " Everything is right, and
we are still on our way to the hospital. Yeah, he came around this
time."

Jesse didn't respond. He knew Vee was right. He had an Aunt
who fought diabetes til it took her life with complications.

They rode to the hospital in silence, only Vee's gentle sobs.

Chapter 18

Jesse pulled in, followed by Maddie and Doris, the Paul with Benny. Max stayed behind to watch the kids.

Jesse and Vee ran to the desk.

" Baylee, they just brought Andy Levesque in. Can you tell us anything?"

The nurse eyed Vee.

" Are you family?" Baylee knew Andy didn't have siblings. They had dated for about a month.

Vee took a deep breath.

" I'm Andy's finance'. "

" I'm sorry, that's not considered family. I really wish I could help."

Baylee really wishes she could.

"Come on, Bay, you know Andy is like a brother to me."

" I do know that Jesse, but you know the rules. I can't."

Meanwhile, the others caught up. One look at Jesse and Vee had everyone talking at once.

Maddie pulled Jesse aside.

" What's wrong?"

Jesse looked lost.

" They can't tell us anything. We are not family."

Maddie went to the desk.

" Baylee, I remember Andy once telling me he made Jesse his emergency contact. It's in his records."

Baylee's fingers flew over the keyboard.

"You're right, Mads. I'll get the doctor for you, Jesse."

The group was quiet while waiting for the doctor. The silence was so loud.. everything seemed amplified, the clock, the desk phone, medical carts.

Finally, the doctor came out.

" Hello, Jesse?"

Jesse gave her a little wave.

" Okay, so, I'm dr. Sanderson, right now, Andy is stable. However, there was a situation in the ambulance that was not good. Andy had gone into cardiac arrest."

Vee fainted, and Benny caught her. An orderly came quickly with a wheelchair. The doctor was sure Vee would come around before continuing. The orderly brought Vee a glass of water.

" Are you okay, Mam?" Vee nodded.

Jesse said to Dr. Sanderson.

" So he had a heart attack ?"

" No, cardiac arrest is not a heart attack. Think of it as an electrical problem that made the heart stop beating."

" That doesn't sound much better," Jesse said.

"Not at all. His heart was shocked back. He will be staying for observation, but he is resting comfortably."

"Can we see him?"

" I'd prefer you just look in at him, not wake him. His body has been through enough. He needs to rest."

Jesse and Vee nodded.

Everyone sat quietly in the waiting room. Vee sat with Paul, leaning against him like she would collapse without him.

"Vee, the doctors, they are doing all they can. Andy's going to be fine. You know he's a fighter."

Vee nodded, even while thinking Andy was not a fighter. He doesn't like arguing and goes out of his way to avoid conflict. He's just a gentle giant.

Dr Sanderson came back, her face none too happy.

"I'm sorry to bring bad news. Andy had another cardiac episode, and this time, it was a heart attack. We are prepping him for surgery. We are going to first do a cardiac cath, then fix what needs to be done."

Once again, the group fell silent. Only Vee's gentle sobbing could be heard.

Benny spoke first.

" This is crazy. The man is a health nut, exercises daily, he is in top shape. It's not fair, just not fair, dammit."

Maddie, whose eyes were shiny, wet, silent tears.

" When I first started working at the paper, Andy was so health conscious, I called him 'Rabbit.'

Then 'Bugs Bunny', which somehow led to 'Bugsy'. He used to get a good laugh out of that."

Jesse laughed.

" Yep, that's Andy, when we played hockey after games, some guys wanted to go to McDonald's or for pizza. Andy dragged us to a restaurant, and he would pay the difference if someone could afford it."

Everyone stayed silent again.

Ray and Frank showed up and joined the group.

Others called, trying to find out news, and the doctor had a nurse come out to let them know Andy was heading into surgery. The nurse also told them she would come out with updates.

Everyone just sat, nobody sure what to say at that moment. It was hard picturing Andy, the one going through this. He's so health-conscious.

Paul, who was still sitting with Vee, strong little Vee. Putting his arm around her shoulders, Paul knew Vee was about to lose it. Vee looked at Paul.

"All I keep thinking of is what if he dies." After a long pause. "What am I supposed to do if Andy dies?"

Paul felt tears behind his eyes.

"Get that out of your head. When it comes down to that, when things come down to that, I stop thinking negatively and only think positive thoughts. Andy is going to be alright. Think positive."

Time crawled by, everyone stayed, and nobody wanted to leave. Steve Lin stopped by with coffee and donuts knowing this group won't even leave the waiting room for a minute. He pulled Paul to the side. " What are they saying?" Paul sighed.

" The only update we got is things are going well, but there's always the risk with diabetes. Poor kid, you spend your whole life being healthy then this, and his girl Vee, she's a train wreck."

Steve nodded. " I get that. If anything happened to Lisa, I have no words.. I'd be just gone.""

Dr Sanderson came out.

Everyone looked up at her. She went over to Jesse but called Vee over to them.

" So Andy is out of surgery, we had ourselves a few setbacks, his glucose levels reached really high then low levels.. but then sort of leveled out. The thing that worried me and my team was his blood pressure also spiked really high. So we will keep monitoring all this and other things. We have a very sick man on our hands, but I am going to say we are going to fix all of that. "The doctor looked at Vee. "Okay, I want you to know that there's no guarantee in life, but I am going to try my hardest to get Andy to a good

place." The doctor looked around the room. " he's very loved."

Vee nodded and then hugged Dr Sanderson. A nurse came out minutes later.

" Andy is in recovery, then he will be going into Cardiac ICU. Once that happens it will be only two family members per visit. We are making an exception, according to dr Sanderson. My advice though, all this is going to take time, I would go home, get some food and rest. He needs you to be strong for him."

Chapter 19

Mostly Everyone had gone home, except Vee, Dorie and Maddie. Vee wasn't leaving, and Maddie and Dorie were not leaving her alone.

The three women sat huddled together, holding hands as if in prayer. Friends by chance, but family through love.

The nurse came back out about an hour later. The three women expected her to tell them two could go in to visit.

" Dr Sanderson was adamant that I tell you of any changes.

Mr Levesque is having another setback. All his levels are extremely high. We are changing his medications again."

" Will he have another heart attack? " Maddie asked.

The nurse took a deep breath.

" At this point, we are looking at so many things. One is organ failure. We really need to get those numbers down."

Vee stood and looked the nurse in the eye.

"Thank you for everything."

" You're welcome, Vee. We are doing everything to get him better."

The nurse left.

"Organ failure?" Vee looked puzzled.

"Vee, listen to me. He doesn't have organ failure. They are looking to prevent that." Maddie held her friend's hand as she said that to her.

Vee shook her head.

" I'm really scared, my mind is racing, my Gosh, I can even see his face."

Dorie nodded. "It's a shock. My whole family went through it when my mom got sick. My dad was a trainwreck even when she was doing better in Chemotherapy. I missed a lot of work. I was so busy helping to get her better. You do what you can. Andy knows you love him, Vee. I think he will fight for you."

Another hour crawled by, and Maddie and Dorie finally convinced Vee to go down to the cafeteria and get something to eat.

" You know, what I don't get?"

Vee said between mouthfuls she was an eater, she wasn't going to pretend, she wasn't famished. Maddie and Dorie looked at her.

" Andy doesn't eat any sugar, no snacks, he does eat home-cooked meals plus he makes his own version of take out foods.

If it's food, what is it?"

" Sugar, Glucose is sneaky, it's in everything, and it doesn't even have to be "bad for you" stuff.

Bread, rice, and pasta all turn to glucose in your body. So being diabetic, it sucks. "

" Andy told me once he found out he had to restrict his diet, he suddenly had cravings like never before," Maddie said.

Vee nodded. " He said the same to me. Like it was a challenge."

"That's terrible. If someone told me, I could have chocolate... I'd go nuts." Dorie said.

" Me too, " Maddie and Vee said together.

The girls finished their meal and headed back up to the waiting room.

The nurse came rushing over. She looked upset.

"Vee, come quickly. Andy is asking for you; he's in ICU, but he has given consent that you are his partner, you're family. Just remember, he just went through major, major surgery, and we are surprised he woke up. He doesn't look so great."

The nurse led her to where Andy was. They got to the room, and Andy was back to being unresponsive.

The nurse, Jenny, said she was hoping he'd still be alert. Of course, it was rare for someone to wake up so soon.

" I'll leave you alone for a few moments. You really need to get some sleep, even if you curl up on chairs in a waiting room. I believe the worse is over. Andy is going to need it when this is all over.

A different nurse came back out,

she told the three ladies, her name was Jewel. Jewel told them Andy was stable at the moment and that they should follow her. Maddie, Vee and Dorie looked at each other, then shrugged. Jewel led them down a long hallway. They entered into an older part of the hospital. She brought them into one of the rooms, which was filled with bunk beds.

"It's technically for drs that wind up doing double shifts. A lot of times, we let patient's families bunk down. We know how hard it is to leave your family. There is a shower and bathroom in the back, extra toothbrushes and lots of trial-size stuff donated from hotels. If there are any changes in Mr Levesque, Andy, I'll let you know. He is stable. Like I said, it's a good thing." Jewel gave them a quick nod and left.

Vee looked around. " Well, that was nice of them. Maybe that's the best idea: get some sleep. Right?"

Maddie and Dorie nodded.

They all showered and went to bed, and sleep came easy. Exhaustion had sunk in. When they woke up, they took quick bathroom trips and went back to the waiting room. Jewel was still there. She came over to them and told them that Andy's numbers were so much better.

He was due to see the dr.. It was only 9 am, Jewel told them to go down and get some breakfast. Dr Sanderson wasn't due to see Andy before 11 am.

The three friends headed to the cafeteria, Vee surprisingly in a better mood, lighter.

" Belgium waffles, let's have that, I haven't had them in ages." Vee said.

Dorie and Maddie looked at each other. Vee laughed and responded to their looks."

" I don't know, I just feel at peace. My head stopped throbbing, my stomach stopped rolling, and my legs weren't shaking. Maybe it's a good sign."

"Well, then, let's get some Belgium waffles for your belly,"

Dorie said, and Maddie nodded in agreement. They got their waffles and coffee, sat down

and talked, and two hours flew by. Heading back to the waiting room, they could not believe their eyes.

STELLA.

Dorie and Maddie grabbed Vee, who had bloodshed in her eyes.

Maddie got in front of Vee.

" She's not worth it. Ignore her, and let's just go wait in the waiting room for Dr Sanderson."

They got to the waiting room, and Stella came up to Vee.

" You might as well go home. Look, Andy loves me. He will come back to me. He's just angry."

Now Dorie had it, she started at Stella, but fortunately, she was grabbed from behind by her big brother, Jesse. His voice was firm. He wasn't the Jesse most were used to.

"What are you here for, Stella?"

"I'm here to see Andy."

"Andy doesn't want to see you."

" You don't know that."

" You know Stella, I'm not used to doing it, but believe me, there are a lot of trumped up charges I can put you away for. "

" Are you threatening me, Sheriff ?"

"No, ma'am."

" I am promising you, if you don't get your ass out of here, I will call in to have you forcibly removed and arrested for harassment. Just so you know, I am well-versed in the law."

Dr Sanderson came down the hallway. " Sit down, Vee."

They all sat.

" I wanted to come out here with good news. He was stable and going forward. But I can't. Andy had a stroke, so now I don't know where we stand. I have to run more tests. He is stable but unresponsive."

Silent tears ran down Vee's face.

" Andy's in a coma?"

" Yes, I'm sorry. I wish I had better news. I'll be running a test. I suggest you all go home and get some rest. "

" Can I see him?"

" Against my better judgment, yes, but please under 5 minutes, there will be someone coming to take him for test."

" Okay"

Vee felt like her legs were made of cement walking behind Jewel.

Jewel felt bad for Vee. She turned and said not to get discouraged. Vee nodded.

When they got to the ICU room Andy was in, Jewel took Vee's hand.

Andy was hooked up on life support. It wasn't what Vee was expecting, so she gasped.

" I thought he was just unresponsive, like in a coma, but.."

Jewel let out a deep breath.

" I can't say a lot, okay, but he just seems to keep going from bad to worse. It could progress, but the doctors could pull him out of it. I'm not trying to give you false hope. "

Vee nodded, moved to Andy's side, Took his hand moved it to her mouth.

" I love you, Andy. I need you to know that. Please come back to me, please."

Silent tears slid down her cheeks. Vee said a prayer. She never asked for anything in life. She never wanted anything more than right now, just for him to say, " Hiya, Babe." Jewel cleared her throat. Vee knew she had to leave but kept hearing the words.. he seemed to be going from bad to worse.

" Don't you dare die on me, Andy Levesque, don't you dare," Vee said as she bent to kiss him goodbye. When she went to drop Andy's hand tho, Vee felt him squeeze her hand.

" Jewel, he squeezed my hand."

Just then, all the machines went haywire. Jewel pushed a rapid response code. The drs flew in the room, and Jewel guided Vee out.

" Jewel, what's happening?"

" I don't know, I thought I saw Andy open his eyes, then you said he squeezed your hand, and the machines went off. Let's get you back to the waiting room."

Vee told Maddie and Dorie what happened, and they decided to go down to the chapel, Andy sure could use more prayers. They let the desk know where they were. Maddie called Jesse to give him an update.

" Me and Dorie are going to stay with Vee, okay? Yeah, I love you too."

Chapter 20

Andy was taken off of life support; he had been floating in and out of consciousness for a week now, but he was stable. Dr Sanderson was hopeful that Andy had been through the worse, but she wasn't sure what damage was done. The staff was running tests that they could and monitoring him around the clock.

"Andy has a long, long recovery, Vee. I cannot even begin to tell you how long because until he actually is awake, I don't know where we stand."

" What kind of damage?"

"In layman's terms, organ failure did damage, heart failure more than likely, brain damage, paralysis, vision or hearing loss.. but again, we don't know anything, at least something, until he wakes up."

"He will wake up, though, right?"

" The only thing we can do is Pray and have faith."

" Yeah, I know, Dr Sanderson. Thank you for everything."

" We will get through this, Vee. He is strong and loved."

A nurse came up to Vee and Dr Sanderson.

" Excuse me, Dr, the patient in room 4 is awake."

Vee and Dr Sanderson looked at each other.

" That's Andy! " Vee squealed.

" Give me a few minutes. I'll come get you."

A few minutes turned into 38 minutes, with Vee going off the wall with anxiety. Dr Sanderson came out very poker-faced. She looked at Vee. Vee sensed it was not good news, but he was awake. I can handle it, she thought to herself. The Dr spoke in a level tone.

" Okay, Andy has no feeling in his left side. He has sight and hearing, but he cannot speak. He may have some loss of recognition."

"Amnesia?"

"Most likely temporary; don't get ahead of yourself. He has a long and I do mean a long road to recovery but he will recover. What comes back to him will be a blessing. He will be here a few more days until we think it's safe for him to enter a rehabilitation center. Would you like to see him? "

" YES!"

" Okay, remember slowly, he may not even be awake now, dozing in and out still, but he is responding to being awakened."

Vee nodded.

When she got to the room door, Vee braced herself for anything.

Her eyes met Andy's, and tears formed. He was so pale and thin-looking, but he was alive. He was alive.

Vee gave Andy a little wave from the doorway, and he waved back.